D0575314

For Thomas and Emily

Cherub Cat,
Angel Tiger

For he is of the tribe of Tiger.
For the Cherub Cat is a term of the Angel Tiger.
For he has the subtlety and hissing of a serpent, which
in goodness he suppresses.
For he will do no destruction, if he is well-fed, neither
will he spit without provocation.
For he purrs in thankfulness, when God tells him he's a
good Cat.
For he is an instrument for the children to learn benevolence
upon.
For every house is incompleat without him and a blessing is lacking in
the spirit.

CHRISTOPHER SMART: *Jubilate Agno*

· MARIE ANGEL ·

Cherub Cat, Angel Tiger

· *A little history of the cat* ·

· PELHAM BOOKS ·

PELHAM BOOKS
Published by the Penguin Group
27 Wrights Lane, London W8 5TZ, England
Viking Penguin Inc., 40 West 23rd Street, New York, New York 10010, USA
Penguin Books Australia Ltd, Ringwood, Victoria, Australia
Penguin Books Canada Ltd, 2801 John Street, Markham, Ontario, Canada L3R 1B4
Penguin Books (NZ) Ltd, 182–190 Wairau Road, Auckland 10, New Zealand

Penguin Books Ltd, Registered Offices: Harmondsworth, Middlesex, England

First published 1988

A CIP catalogue record for this book is available from the British Library.

ACKNOWLEDGEMENTS
The author is grateful to Jonathan Cape Ltd for permission to use an extract from *Down the Garden Path* by Beverley Nichols (first published 1932).

Made and printed in Italy by Olivotto

Typeset by Wilmaset, Birkenhead, Wirral

Contents

Neither Friend Nor Servant

Cat said: 'I am not a friend, and I am not a servant. I am the cat who walks by himself, and I wish to come into your cave.'
RUDYARD KIPLING: *Just So Stories* (1902)

The cat is unique in that it is the only domestic animal that has been tamed on its own terms. It is still the same animal that made friends with man some thousands of years ago. It has the same reserve, the same independence, and is as self-sufficient and self-reliant as its wild ancestors. Even the cosiest of cats is in harmony with its wild nature.

But as every cat-lover knows, cats are soft, gentle, affectionate creatures, their grace and beauty a source of constant pleasure. The cat may not be a social animal, lacking the dog's easy tolerance of human foibles and frailties, yet its relationship with its owner, its human companion, is trusting, playful, loving and is akin to that of a kitten with its mother.

The cat is a great individualist, full of contradictions; and it is this ambiguity, the fierce tiger in the gentle tabby, that is part of the attractiveness of such a magnetic and mercurial creature.

Cat and Mouse

The beaste is called a Musion, for that he is enimie to Myse and Rattes. And he is called a Catte of the Greeks because he is slye and wittie: for that he seeth so sharpely, that he overcommeth darkness of the nighte, by the shyninge lyghte of his eyne.

JOHN BOSSEWELL: *Workes of Armorie* (1576)

An animal as fascinating as the cat has inevitably been the subject of many creation myths and in nearly all of them God creates the cat to be the enemy of the mouse. Indeed, the mouse is usually the work of the Devil.

In one story the Devil sneaks on board the Ark disguised as a mouse; when Noah discovers him gnawing a hole in the timbers, he throws his fur glove at him and as the glove falls, it is transformed into a cat, the four fingers becoming its legs and the thumb its tail. In an Arabic version of the Ark story, Noah is at his wits' end to stop the mice eating up the stores and annoying the other passengers. In despair, he consults the lion. The noble beast listens in silence and then sneezes – not once, but twice – and from his nostrils spring two miniature lions. Immediately, the cats pounce upon the mice and devour them.

Curiously, for such a beautiful animal, a surprising number of legends attribute its birth to some form of miscegenation. According to a Chinese legend, for example, the cat was the result of the lioness's infidelity with the monkey.

The cat's Darwinian, as opposed to its mythic, origins is thought to be *miacis*, a weasel-like creature alive at the same time as the dinosaur and a common ancestor not only of all cats, large and small, but of all carnivorous mammals. It took millions of years for cat-like creatures to evolve and differentiate into the many species known today. Yet the gulf between fact and fiction, science and myth, may not be as great as it would at first appear. Mice *did* play an important part in the evolution of cats, for it was the plentiful supply of small rodents as prey that made feline evolution possible. In the legends, the story-teller's imagination has anticipated scientific discovery and condensed many millions of years of evolution into one dramatic flash.

A *Familiar and* Well *Knowne Beaste*

A *Catte is a familiar and well knowne beaste.* O*nce cattes were all wilde, but afterward they retyred to houses.*
EDWARD TOPSELL: *The* Historie *of* Four-*Footed* Beastes (1607)

The domestic cat traces its ancestry back to a small African wild cat, *Felis sylvestris lybica*, a shy nocturnal hunter and the only biddable member of the cat family. Its first known home was some 5000 years ago, in Ancient Egypt, although wild cats of various kinds were probably tamed for hunting and kept in some form of captivity by primitive peoples much earlier.

Attracted by the rats in the Egyptians' granaries, the wild cats came unbidden to feast, but stayed as welcome guests. For the Egyptians realised that this was the beginning of a mutually beneficial relationship and trust and affection slowly developed between cat and man. The Egyptians were skilled at taming wild animals, and soon the cat entered the Egyptian household not only as a formidable mouser but also as a loved pet. Eventually, so powerful was its hold on the Egyptian imagination, it was worshipped as a deity.

In Egypt the natural death of a cat was marked by mourning and the ritual shaving of the eyebrows of the household. The killing of a cat, whether intentional or not, was punishable by death. Cats were mummified as were their owners when they died, and placed in cases made from woven straw, wood or bronze; often the cat heads of the mummy cases had eyes inlaid with gold and silver, lapis lazuli and obsidian. There were special cat cemeteries, the most famous at Bubastis, a shrine of the cat goddess.

As a result of archaeological interest in Egypt in the nineteenth century, 180,000 mummies from the cat cemetery at Beni Hassan were shipped to Liverpool in 1890 and sold as fertiliser or curios: heads sold for 4s 6d (23p) and bodies for 5s 6d (28p). Only one of these mummies found its way to the British Museum in London.

Although no longer sacred, the cat is still a cult object and central to the emotional lives of very many people. Doctors acknowledge the therapeutic value of keeping a cat, for stroking its fur helps to reduce high blood pressure.

The Diminutive Lyon

All cats were at first wild, but were at length tamed by the industry of Mankind; it is a Beast of prey, even the tame one, more especially the wild, it being in the opinion of many nothing but a diminutive Lyon.
WILLIAM S SALMON: *The Compleat English Physician* (1693)

The modern domestic cat – *Felis catus* – is a small member of the Felidae, or cat family. Its cousins include the tiger, the largest of the large cats, and the rusty-spotted cat, which is smaller than the domestic cat.

The Felidae is divided into three genera: the *Panthera*, with the six large cats (tiger, lion, leopard, snow and clouded leopards and the jaguar): the *Felis*, containing all the small cats; and the *Acinonyx*, with only one member, the cheetah, classed separately because it is the only cat with non-retractable claws.

Wild cats are native to all parts of the world except Australia, whose indigenous 'cats', such as the tiger cat, evolved much earlier than the modern cats and are really marsupials, since they carry their young in pouches.

Wild cats are superbly adapted in evolutionary terms to their place in the natural order. Many of them have developed special characteristics to suit their way of life: the African sand cat, for example, has dense mats of fur to protect its pads from scorching sand and rock. Wild cats are threatened with extinction not from natural causes, through failure to maintain themselves in the food chain, but because the beauty of their fur has attracted the lethal attention of human hunters.

Cheetah Pampas Cat
Margay
Puma Lion
Sand Cat

Although the American continent is rich in wild cat species – some such as the Bobcat, Jaguar, Jaguarundi, Margay, Ocelot and Puma are found only in the New World – no wild cat has been tamed into domesticity. There is some evidence that in the past native American Indians trained small wild cats to hunt, but the first domestic cats were immigrants along with the Pilgrim Fathers. The American Shorthair, a working tabby, is regarded as the closest to the seventeenth-century cat, although as a pedigree breed it was only developed this century.

In the United States some wild cats are kept as pets, particularly the ocelot, the most tameable of the small wild cats. There is a national club for owners of exotic cats, the Long Island Ocelot Club, which includes margays, jaguarundis and bobcats, as well as ocelots, and even the mountain lion. Although they cannot compete, ocelots are sometimes exhibited at cat shows.

At the first British show at Crystal Palace in 1871, a European wild cat was exhibited, but it proved so ferocious it could not be moved from its travelling cage. The domestic cat is still capable of breeding with the wild cat and in Scotland interbreeding of wild and feral cats (domestic cats gone wild) has been so extensive that some authorities believe the pure-bred Scottish wild cat (the only wild cat in the British Isles) to be very rare.

The European wild cat (*Felis sylvestris*) and the African wild cat (*Felis sylvestris lybica*), the ancestor of the domestic cat, are now regarded as extremes of the same species, not separate ones as was once thought. In one respect, however, they are very different, for the aggressive and unpredictable nature of the European wild cat makes it virtually untameable.

The Immortal Cat

The beautiful cat endures and endures
GRAVE INSCRIPTION: *Thebes*

In the animistic religion of Ancient Egypt, the curled-up cat was a symbol of eternity, a circle with no beginning and no end. The 75 Praises of Ra, inscribed on royal tombs at Thebes, proclaimed Ra the creator cat-god to be 'the great cat, the avenger of the gods, the judge of words . . . the governor of the holy circle'. Ra represented good against evil and every day at dawn he slew the snake of darkness. Ra's female counterpart was Bast, a fertility goddess, usually represented as a woman with a cat's head and kittens at her feet. Bast was worshipped at various shrines throughout Egypt and her temple cats were sacred.

As the cat spread into other Mediterranean countries, it became associated with various deities – Greek and Roman – and its power, particularly as a fertility symbol, survived the demise of both Egyptian culture and later the classical world. By medieval times the cat was part of a confusion of myths and beliefs that made up the 'Old Religion', a pagan survival particularly strong among superstitious country people.

By a tragic irony, the cat's former power made it vulnerable to persecution. Powerless to defend themselves, thousands of cats were sacrificed in Europe each year after the harvest in the belief that they would bring fertility to the soil and good fortune to the harvesters. In France, the king himself took part in a ceremonial burning of cats that was a mixture of sport and superstition in the Place de Grève on the eve of the feast of St John the Baptist. Louis XIV was the last king to take part in 1648, but the ceremony itself continued into the eighteenth century.

Today, all that survives from this mystic past is the cat as an emblem of good luck, typically a white cat in the East and a black cat in Britain, although in some European countries, such as Italy and Portugal, white cats bring good fortune and black cats the reverse.

The Devil's Familiar

a harmless necessary cat
SHAKESPEARE: *The Merchant of Venice* (1600)

In a list of irrational fears, of things that some men cannot abide, Shylock included the 'harmless necessary cat'. For at the same time as cats were being sacrificed by believers in the old religion, they fell victim to its opponents and were caught up in the hysterical witch hunts that swept Protestant countries. Once the enemy of the snake, the cat was now seen as the 'furred serpent', the familiar of the devil.

Christian zealots who accused defenceless old women of witchcraft were themselves unconsciously demonstrating their own belief in the power of the old religion, for witches were derived from the shamans and shamankas, the wise men and women of Nordic mythology. Cats were often depicted as their companions as they were of the fertility goddesses, Frigg and Freyja. For a long time the old and the new religions existed side-by-side: there are even wall paintings in Schleswig Cathedral of Frigg riding on a broomstick and Freyja astride an enormous striped wild cat.

Such was the hysteria that at its height a cat had only to slip out of a window at night or miaow too loudly or often, for its owner to be accused of witchcraft, ending in death and destruction for them both.

Practical Cats

The worth of a kitten, from the night it is kittened until it shall open its eyes, is a legal penny.
And from the time that it shall kill mice, twopence.
And after it shall kill mice, four legal pence; and so it always remains.
WALES: *The Vendotian Code* (10th century)

Today, although the cat has a secure place in the affections of countless cat-lovers the world over, he no longer has the important practical role of the past, when his skills as a mouser earned him the protection of the law in some societies. In so far as the law recognises him today, it is to acknowledge his continuing wild nature and to absolve him and his owner from responsibility for his actions.

However, at the height of medieval persecution, not even the cat's usefulness saved him from the persecution of credulous peasants and religious bigots. Cats, as well as other animals, were brought before courts of law in France and some were even executed for their 'misdeeds'. The English joke that became a proverbial saying of the Puritan who was seen

Hanging of his cat on Monday
For killing of a rat on Sunday

had a bitter truth for some poor cats.

Cyprus Cats

The best are such as are of a fair and large kind, and of an Exquisite Tabby colour, called Cyprus Cats.
WILLIAM S SALMON: *The Compleat English Physician* (1693)

In East Anglia 'Cyprus Cat' is still the old country name for a tabby. Why 'Cyprus' must remain one of the mysteries of the cat, but 'tabby' is said to derive from Attibiya, a district of Baghdad where watered silk of a pattern similar to the tabby's striped coat was woven.

The subtle beauty of the tabby's coat is achieved by bands of colour, called 'agouti', on *each* hair, not by hairs of different colours. There are three types of tabby pattern: striped, blotched and spotted.

Of the three, the striped or mackerel pattern is the oldest, deriving from the cat's wild ancestry. The blotched originated in Elizabethan England during the sixteenth century and has become not only the dominant tabby pattern but the dominant coat pattern for all cats. The blotched is also known as the classic pattern, since Linnaeus, the great Swedish naturalist who devised the system of scientific classification of plants and animals, classified the blotched tabby as the typical *Felis catus*. The third pattern – the spotted tabby – is also of ancient origin, but is now best seen in pedigree cats, such as the Silver Spotted Shorthair and the Oriental Spotted Tabby.

Cats Of Divers Colours

Cats are of divers colours, but for the most part gryseld
like to congealed yse.
EDWARD TOPSELL: *The Historie of* Foure-Footed *Beastes* (1607)

Chance mutation over the centuries produced a number of different colours and colour combinations from the original tabby. Black, blue, white and red cats have been known in Britain at least since medieval times.

Black was one of the earliest mutations to emerge. Black cats characteristically show a few white hairs and have green eyes. However, modern breed standards now demand that the pedigree black cat should have copper or orange eyes and a jet black coat without any white hairs.

Blue cats are greyish-blue in colour, the 'blue' being genetically a dilute form of black. In the seventeeth century the English antiquarian John Aubrey wrote that the 'common English cat is white with some blewish piedness', but cats with coats of a solid blue were also known. In France, records show that the monks at the monastery of La Grande Chartreuse were breeding blue cats as early as 1558. Until very recently the Chartreuse and the British Blue were regarded as separate breeds, but they are now judged by the same standard. In Britain, the British Blue Shorthair with its beautiful, dense, blue coat and gentle disposition is one of the most popular breeds today.

White cats are genetically white, not albinos. Blue-eyed white cats were once thought to be dull and stupid until it was realised that many of them were deaf.

Red cats are more popularly known as ginger, orange or marmalade cats. Charles Darwin, the naturalist and author of *The Origin of Species*, thought that the ginger tom and the tortoiseshell were male and female of the same variety. In fact, ginger cats can be male or female, and although the tortoiseshell is indeed a female-only variety – the few males born have been sterile – she does not necessarily have to mate with a red-coated cat to produce some tortoiseshell kittens in the litter.

Shorthaired tortoiseshell cats have been pets and working cats, particularly on farms, for centuries. The tortoiseshell-and-white cat is called the Chintz cat in Britain and the Calico cat in the United States.

The tortoiseshell, with its brilliant red, cream and black coat, and its shy, gentle nature, is one of the most sought after of cats. Chance, rather than selective breeding, produced this beautiful cat, and even today with all the sophisticated knowledge at the breeder's disposal, it is difficult to breed to order.

Witty And Whimsical Cats

The cat is an unfaithful domestic, and kept only from the necessity we find of opposing him to the domestics still more incommodius, and which cannot be hunted: for we value not those people who, being fond of all brutes, foolishly keep cats for their amusement.
GEORGES DE BUFFON: *Histoire Naturelle* (1791)

Cats survived the excesses of superstitious persecution and by the eighteenth century their relationship with man had achieved some sort of equilibrium. Many were still illtreated, but official public cruelty was a thing of the past. Young men might still roam the streets looking for cats to shoot for 'sport', but it was not condoned by society.

Literary cat-lovers abounded: from Horace Walpole (whose cat Selima Thomas Gray made immortal in his poem 'On the death of a favourite cat, drowned in a tub of goldfishes'), Robert Southey, Leigh Hunt, to Wordsworth, Shelley and Swinburne. The frail and consumptive Keats fought a butcher's boy for nearly an hour in the street for tormenting a kitten. Christopher Smart, confined to Bedlam when his sanity collapsed, wrote a fine and moving poem about his cat Jeoffrey, his companion in that appalling and inhumane institution.

The cat now was fast becoming a vehicle for wit. The philosopher Jeremy Bentham called his cat Sir John Langborn and invited him to eat macaroni at his table. In the story as recounted by John Bowring, Sir John gave up his giddy youth and 'became sedate and thoughtful – took to the church, laid down his knightly title, and was installed as the Reverend John Langborn. He gradually obtained a great reputation for sanctity and learning, and a Doctor's degree was conferred on him. When I knew him, in his declining days, he bore no other name than the Reverend Doctor John Langborn; and he was alike conspicuous for his gravity and philosophy. Great respect was invariably shown his reverence: and it was supposed he was not far off from a mitre, when old age interfered with hopes and honours.'

Calvin, a Blue Shorthair, who had 'the most irreproachable morals I ever saw thrown away in a cat', was also used by his owner, the American Charles Dudley Warner, as a foil for literary wit in his book *My Summer in a Garden*. But Calvin was truly a cat of character and in the Memoir that Warner wrote after the death of the cat whose 'coat was the finest and softest I have ever seen, a shade of quiet Maltese', Calvin's individuality is described with a loving sincerity that allows him to be himself: 'His friendship was rather constant than demonstrative . . . he liked companionship, but he wouldn't be petted, or fussed over, or sit in any one's lap a moment; he always extricated himself from such familiarity with dignity and with no show of temper. If there was any petting to be done, however, he chose to do it. Often he would sit looking at me, and then, moved by a delicate affection, come and pull at my coat and sleeve until he could touch my face with his nose, and then go away contented.'

Fancy Cats

I conceived the idea that it would be well to hold Cat Shows, so that different breeds, colours, markings, etc might be more carefully attended to, and the domestic cat sitting in front of the fire would then possess a beauty and an attractiveness to its owner unobserved and unknown because uncultivated before.
HARRISON WEIR: *Our Cats* (1889)

Harrison Weir, a noted artist and a fellow of the Royal Horticultural Society, organised the first cat show in London at the Crystal Palace in 1871. Cats had been exhibited before, but simply as fairground attractions, to entertain or amaze the crowd, not with the serious intention of judging for breeding excellence and placing them in an order of merit.

RUSSIAN BLUE
MANX
CHINCHILLA PERSIAN
BEST IN SHOW
BEST OF BREED
SEAL-POINT SIAMESE
BROWN TABBY

Although interest in unusual cats had been growing for some time – stimulated by the exotic feline discoveries travellers had brought back from Turkey and the Far East – most of the cats on show were native British shorthairs. However, the exotic cats won most of the prizes, for a Manx, a 'French-African', Siamese and Persian cats were among the winners. A British cat won the prize for the biggest in the show.

The show was an overnight success. Patronised by Queen Victoria, who owned two blue Persians, cat shows became fashionable. The cat had at last come into his own again. Such was the interest in 'fancy cats' that the National Cat Club was founded in 1887 to organise shows, and keep a stud book and register of cats. Harrison Weir was the first President but later resigned in protest that so many of the Cat Fancy cared more about winning prizes than the welfare of cats.

Cat shows soon became popular in Europe and the United States, where the first show was held in 1895 at Madison Square Garden in New York.

Today over a hundred different pedigree breeds have been standardised and registered with official cat associations in Britain, Europe and the United States. However, these breed standards are not uniform: some standards vary so much that it would be impossible for the same cat to be champion of its breed in both Britain and the United States.

In Great Britain the Governing Council of the Cat Fancy (GCCF) is the official body. The United States has nine recognised official associations, of which the Cat Fanciers' Association (CFA) is one of the most prestigious.

The Perfect Cat

Points of Excellence
HARRISON WEIR: *Standards for Judging Show Cats* (1871)

At the first shows, cats were classified by colour rather than breed or type. Today the Governing Council of the Cat Fancy divides cats into four general categories – short or long coats, British or Foreign – before subdividing into breeds.

The oldest breeds in Britain are descendants of the shorthaired cats that arrived in the baggage of the Roman army. Chance matings between the domestic cat and the European Wild Cat, it is thought, have produced the characteristic round head, sturdy body and thick tail that distinguishes the British Shorthair from cats of Foreign type, which are closer in build to the original domesticated cat.

The first cats in Europe with longhaired coats were the white angoras from Turkey. Explorers brought them back as curiosities to Italy and France during the sixteenth century. When they arrived in Britain from Paris, they were known as 'French cats'.

Later, in the nineteenth century, travellers brought back from Asia Minor the 'Persian' cat, with its even more luxuriant coat of long, thick fur. For a time, all longhaired cats were called 'Persian', as they still are in the United States, although in Britain the official term is now simply 'longhaired'.

'Foreign' cats, such as the Siamese and the Russian Blue, also arrived in Britain in the mid-nineteenth century. The first Siamese were Seal-points with squints and kinks in their tails. (According to legend, a princess threaded her rings on her cat's tail when she went bathing; she kinked the tail to stop them slipping off.) As sacred temple cats they could be owned only by the royal court of Siam; one or two were given to British diplomats or visiting dignitaries, and from these cats the many modern varieties have been bred. The Russian Blue was known as the Archangel cat after the sea-port from which it began its journey to Britain. At first it was shown with the British Blue, but it is now recognised as a separate breed.

American breeders have also made major contributions to the roll-call of pedigree cats. The Maine Coon, a typically American cat, was bred in New England during the latter half of the nineteenth century, and is a tough working cat adapted to harsh weather conditions and similar to the Norwegian Forest Cat. The Burmese, the Japanese Bobtail and the Egyptian Mau were also first developed as breeds in the United States.

Of course, perfection is in the eye of the beholder; and many a moggie-owner prefers the 'natural breeding' of Harrison Weir's 'ordinary garden cat'.

Cats and Kittens

The way Dinah washed her children's faces was this: first she held the poor thing down by its ear with one paw, and then with the other paw she rubbed its face all over, the wrong way, beginning at the nose: and just now, as I said, she was hard at work on the white kitten, which was lying quite still and trying to purr – no doubt feeling that it was meant for its own good.

LEWIS CARROLL: *Through the Looking-glass* (1871)

Kittens are born blind, helpless and totally dependent upon their mothers. Without her absolute devotion few of them would survive.

In the wild, young kittens are preyed upon by many animals, often by those that they will themselves hunt when adult. Wild cats protect their young by changing the site of the nest: they never leave their kittens where they have been born, but laboriously carry them one at a time in their mouths to a new nest. This instinct is still strong in the domestic cat, who continues to move her kittens around to protect them from imaginary dangers.

Mother cats wash their kittens thoroughly, even aggressively, from the moment they are born. This is also essential to survival, for without the stimulus of their mother's tongue they do not urinate. When they are about three weeks old, kittens start to wash themselves and each other – if not very efficiently – and by the time they are six weeks old they can clean their paws, faces and tails properly.

Washing is very important to cats. Not only do they wash themselves after eating and to keep their coats clean, they seem also to groom themselves for comfort and in some circumstances as a defence mechanism. For a cat that has tried to do something and failed – to jump onto a high wall, for example – will usually sit down and carefully wash its coat as though it were a matter of absolute indifference whether it got over the wall or not. Similarly, cats in a situation that is difficult for them to cope with – being teased or talked about – will often sit down and groom themselves.

Skittish Cats

I am sure that cats have a strong sense of fun, and, like children, love the delights of make-believe. Two of them will meet on the lawn, and with ears set back and lashing tails will play at having a mortal combat. In the fiercest of the fray, when the limbs of the wrestlers are locked in deadly fight, they will suddenly stop and lick each other's faces . . . A mother-pussy lashes her tail for her kitten to play with, looking round out of the corner of her eye to see if he is taking notice. A small kitten, just learning to mouse, will toss up a ball of wool or a bit of fur and make an imaginary mouse of it.

GERTRUDE JEKYLL: Home and Garden (1900)

Games play an important part in the lives of both cats and kittens. Mother cats teach their kittens how to catch prey by playing hunting games; adult cats keep their skills honed by pretending that a piece of string is a snake or a ball of wool a mouse.

Although chase and pounce are instinctive, it seems that kittens have to be taught to be good hunters. The best mousers, for example, are usually cats that have been instructed in the art as kittens by their mothers bringing them live prey. However, kittens that are brought up on amicable terms with one of their natural prey – a mouse or a bird perhaps – are less likely to hunt others of the same species when they are adult.

One of the pleasures of living with a cat is sharing its fun and frolics, although sometimes a cat's sheer *joie de vivre* can be disconcerting. Norman Davey, in *The Hungry Traveller in France*, for instance, tells the charming story of the cat in the Brasserie Liègeoise in Boulogne: 'Visitors staying in the house should not fail to make themselves acquainted with Madame's cat. This is an engaging animal that swings by its legs, with remarkable velocity, around a revolving hat-stand. It is an entertaining exhibition; but not one to be recommended to the diner who has taken a *fine* or two over the stipulated eight. He may be led to ascribe the phenomenon to his state of health.'

Cat Lore

True Calendars, as Pusses eare
Washt o're, to tell what change is neare.
ROBERT HERRICK: *His Age* (1648)

Old country lore, as here recorded by Robert Herrick in the seventeenth century, attributed to the cat the ability to forecast the weather. A cat washing behind its ears indicates rain; if it sits with its back to the fire, a frost. If a cat sleeps with all four paws under its body, it will be cold; if it sleeps stretched out at full length, it will be warm. A cat sleeping with its front paws covering its nose foretells high winds.

As with many old country beliefs based on a close and accurate observation of natural phenomena, there is some truth in cats washing before storms. The cat's soft, dry fur is naturally full of latent electricity. The atmospheric conditions before a storm make its coat increasingly uncomfortable and by licking the fur the cat is able to reduce the unpleasant currents running through it.

To seafarers black cats are unlucky, bringing bad weather and disaster. Tortoiseshell cats are considered lucky and in the Far East sailors send them up the mast to put the storm devils to flight. On land also the tortoiseshell traditionally brings luck: in Scotland good health to the house it lives in and in England second sight to those who play with it.

In Europe and the East, white cats are as lucky as black cats are to English-speaking peoples. And in China cats are kept in shops as good luck charms: the older and uglier the cat, the more luck it will bring its owner.

The Garden Cat

. . . a large and ravishing Persian cat was clearly visible in my back yard, patting my only geranium with a verve which would have been more fittingly reserved for a mouse.
BEVERLEY NICHOLS: *Down the Garden Path* (1932)

For many people cats and gardens are poor mixers. Being territorial animals, cats like to appropriate gardens whether or not they have valid claim – which can cause a surge of conflicting emotions in even the cat-lover. Beverley Nichols, equally passionate about gardens as cats, devised an ingenious and novel method of deterring them: he poured small pools of treacle on the walls surrounding his town garden.

Gertrude Jekyll, who made garden design into an art, always had three or four cats – usually tabby, or tabby and white – and was amused rather than upset by their antics in the garden: 'Pinkieboy has his own jungle, a small thicket close to the house . . . with an undergrowth of Cistus, Bracken, and long grass. He makes regular lairs, that retain their shape, and look like grassy tunnels. The little nieces call them the Pussy-lie-downs.' Pinkieboy was one of Gertrude Jekyll's favourites, a big heavy cat, silver tabby and white, who would make a stately advance down one of the turf rides to meet her before making a bow and offering the softest fur of 'his beautifully-kept white waistcoat and shirt-front' for her kind stroking.

Calvin, the Maltese cat who added to the liveliness of Charles Dudley Warner's *My Summer in a Garden*, 'delighted, above all things, to accompany me walking about the garden, hearing the birds, getting the smell of the fresh earth, and rejoicing in the sunshine . . . If I worked, he sat and watched me, or looked off over the bank, and kept his ear open to the twitter in the cherry-trees.'

'Rusticus' in *The Field* recorded the story of the anonymous white Persian with a strange addiction: 'I have also come across an instance of a white blue-eyed Persian cat which had a strong affection for the blossom of the pink sweet-pea, and would jump on the table to search vases of flowers for her favourite morsel – often with disastrous results. Later on this same cat found rows of sweet-peas in a walled garden, and her industry became unbounded. If pink sweet-peas were not to be had, she would eat other light-coloured flowers of that species, but never the dark ones, nor would she touch any other flower.'

The Celestial Cat

How can we be interested in an animal that did not know how to achieve a place in the night sky, where all the animals scintillate, from the bear and dog to the lion, the bull, the ram and the fish?
VOLTAIRE (1694-1778)

The twelve zodiacal constellations are very old, deriving from the sympathetic magic of the early hunters; to them the smaller members of the cat family were of no interest, either as prey or predator, and they had no need to try to control them by magic. It is not surprising, therefore, that the little cats – and the domestic version probably did not even then exist – are not among the stars.

Voltaire, in his indifference to cats, is unusual among modern thinkers and philosophers. When Montaigne shut himself away in his tower of contemplation the only creature allowed to disturb him was his cat; and his respect for her was such that it lead him to conjecture: 'when I play with my cat, who knows whether she is not amusing herself more with me than I with her?' Dr Johnson, the great lexicographer, fed his cat Hodge on oysters; and fearing that his servants might resent running errands for a cat and take it out on the poor creature, he would himself go out specially to buy them.

During Voltaire's lifetime two astronomers did try to establish a place for the cat in the sky. Johann Bode, Director of the Berlin Observatory, proposed Felis as a constellation in 1775, as did Joseph Lalande, a Frenchman responsible for many star catalogues and who regarded his discovery as the summation of his life's work: 'I love cats, I adore cats, and may be forgiven for putting one in the sky after sixty years of hard work.' Sadly, neither constellation is accepted today.

But as an emblem of the moon, the cat has always been a celestial creature. It was once thought that the pupils of its eyes enlarged and contracted as the moon itself waxed and waned. And even today, cats are thought to be moon-struck, a full moon in some mysterious way drawing them irresistibly out at night.

Ship's Cat

So when the painted ship
Sailed through a golden sunrise on the Thames
A grey tail waved upon the misty poop
And Whittington had his venture out at sea.
ALFRED NOYES: *Tales of the Mermaid Tavern* (1913)

While its wild cousins retreat further and further into the North African desert, the domestic cat has voyaged triumphantly round the world.

In medieval and modern times, cats travelled from Europe to the Americas and Australia as emigrants with missionaries and the first settlers.

In the ancient world, Phoenician sailors were responsible for spreading the black cat, one of the first mutations, around the Mediterranean. Similarly, the blotched tabby that emerged in Elizabethan England owes its world-wide dominance to the former supremacy of the British navy. For sailors, as Noah before them, know that a cat on board is essential to control unruly rodents and the more adventurous among the feline crew sometimes jumped ship in foreign ports and established their own 'colonies'.

The Manx cat is not native to the Isle of Man, but arrived there when it was shipwrecked off the coast. Tailless cats originated in the Middle East, and the 'Manx' is thought to have been cargo on one of the Spanish ships that foundered in the great storm that scattered the Armada after its defeat by Drake in 1688.

There are many stories similar to the Dick Whittington legend in European folklore where a cat is sent over the seas to be traded in a foreign land and brings his owner fortune by ridding an Eastern prince of the mice that have overrun his palace. Sadly though, the cat that brought Whittington fame and fortune was probably not a puss at all: for Whittington made his fortune as a mercer, a dealer in bonds; the common term for a bond at that time was the French *achat*, pronounced 'cat' by the English; it is easy to see how in the telling and retelling of the story of the poor boy who became three times Lord Mayor of London that the nature of his 'cat' should undergo a sea change.

The Fishing Cat

The catte wyll fyshe eate, but she wyl not her feete wette
TAVERNER: *Proverbs* (1539)

The cat's proverbial love of fish and dislike of water have been enshrined as fact by many naturalists. In *The Natural History of Selborne* Gilbert White, noted for the accuracy of his observation unlike the more credulous earlier 'naturalists' such as Topsell and Salmon, wrote that cats have a 'violent fondness for fish . . . yet nature in this instance seems to have planted in them an appetite that, unassisted, they know not how to gratify'.

Yet there are many recorded instances to the contrary: Erasmus Darwin knew of a cat that fished for trout in a deep millpool and W H Hudson in *A Shepherd's Life* recorded the story of another trout fisher: 'He was a very large, handsome, finely marked tabby, with a thick coat, and always appeared very well nourished but never wanted to be fed. He was a nice-tempered, friendly animal, and whenever he came in he appeared pleased at seeing the inmates of the house, and would go from one to the other, rubbing his sides against their legs and purring aloud with satisfaction. Then they would give him food, and he would take a morsel or two or lap up as much milk as would fill a teaspoon and leave the rest. He was not hungry, and it always appeared, they said, as if he smelt at or tasted the food they put down for him just to please them.

'At the back of the cottage there was a piece of waste ground extending to the river, with a small, old ruinous barn standing on it a few yards from the bank. Between the barn and the stream the ground was overgrown with rank weeds, and here one day Caleb (the shepherd) came by chance

upon his cat eating something among the weeds – a good-sized, fresh-caught trout! . . . They did not destroy their favourite, nor tell anyone of their discovery, but they watched him and found that it was his habit to bring a trout every day to that spot, but how he caught his fish was never known.'

Some modern authorities attribute the cat's supposed dislike of water to its North African wild origins and desert habitat. Yet the cat family as a whole takes easily to water: tigers will swim across sea channels; in South America both the jaguar and the ocelot are good swimmers; and in Asia the Fishing Cat has partially webbed feet to adapt it to water.

Indeed, one modern breed of domestic cat, the Turkish Van, which is closely related to the Angora, loves bathing and swimming. Perhaps its truer to say that cats are not averse to water if they choose it for themselves.

Helpful Cats

The cat is not quite so unsocial a creature as some naturalists would have us believe. He is able to take thought for other cats and for his human companion – master hardly seems the right word in the case of such an animal – who is doubtless to him only a very big cat that walks erect on his hind-legs.
W H HUDSON: *A Shepherd's Life* (1910)

Georges de Buffon in his *Histoire Naturelle* gave the traditional view of cats when he wrote: 'They easily assume the habits of society, but never acquire its manners; for they have only the appearance of attachment or friendship . . . the cat appears to have no feelings which are not interested, to have no affection that is not conditional, and to carry on no intercourse with men, but with the view of turning it to his own advantage.'

The cat is by nature a solitary hunter, not given to sharing its prey, and of necessity self-reliant. Yet many cats bring 'gifts' home to their owners, only to have the tenderly presented mouse or bird roughly rejected and themselves soundly scolded for their 'cruelty'.

But in less prosperous times, cats have been thanked for their generosity by grateful recipients, some of whom have actually been saved from starvation. There is the celebrated story of Sir Henry Wyat, slowly dying of hunger in the Tower of London: a friendly cat began bringing him pigeons through his cell window, and Wyat was able to persuade his gaoler to cook them for him. And Elizabeth Hard, one of the first Quaker settlers in Philadelphia in the seventeenth century, has recorded her despair and desperation as she tried to make a meal from the few remaining dry biscuits, the last of the provisions she and her husband had brought with them, when, miraculously, her pet cat suddenly returned from hunting and laid a rabbit at her feet.

W H Hudson himself in A *Shepherd's Life* gives many examples of generous cats – from the white cat of a woodman in Savernake Forest who would bring in a partridge and lay it on the kitchen floor to the cat in Argentina who would daily present his owner with a tinamou from the pampas for his dinner. And a few years ago in Cornwall a Convent of Poor Clares had a cat that brought rabbits to the Mother Abbess. The convent dogs also knew of the cat's habit and tried to waylay it and steal its prize; but the cat would outwit them and on occasion even tried to bring the rabbit into the kitchen through the pantry window!

Strange Friends

The cat, like many other animals, will often form singular attachments. One would sit in my horse's manger and purr and rub his nose, which undoubtedly the horse enjoyed, for he would frequently turn his head purposely to be so treated . . . while another would cosset up close to a sitting hen, and allow her fresh-hatched chickens to seek warmth by creeping under her. Again, they will rear other animals such as rats, squirrels, rabbits, puppies, hedgehogs; and, when motherly inclined, will take to almost anything, even to a young pigeon.

HARRISON WEIR: *Our Cats* (1889)

There are many stories of the strange friendships that spring up between the cat and other creatures – often with what would be its prey under normal circumstances. Cats deprived of their kittens seem the most susceptible to such odd relationships. Gilbert White recounted the story of the cat who mothered foundling leverets; and there is another story of a cat attempting to feed a young lark.

Usually, it is the cat that makes the first overtures. Mark Twain in *The Innocents Abroad* wrote of the famous friendship between a cat and an elephant in the Marseilles zoo: 'This cat had a fashion of climbing up the elephant's hind legs, and roosting on his back. She would sit up there, with her paws curved under her breast, and sleep in the sun half the afternoon. It used to annoy the elephant at first, and he would reach up and take her down, but she would go aft and climb up again. She persisted until she finally conquered the elephant's prejudices, and now they are inseparable friends.'

It is, however, unwise to attempt to foster such friendships. There is the sad tale of the Chinese Empress who boasted of the friendship between her pet cat and her parrot. She invited the court to watch them feeding together, but the cat got bored and hungry, and unable to wait any longer, ate the parrot for breakfast.

Familiar and Privileged Guest

Bella jumped down, and went through her private cat-door
M SUMMERTON:
Small Wilderness (1959)

The *Oxford English Dictionary Supplement* cites Bella's 'private cat-door' as the first recorded use of the word, but the cat door or flap is not a modern invention. Isaac Newton's consideration was such that he had two holes – one large and one small – cut in his door for his cat and her kitten. In France, a *chatière* in the doors to the *salon* was a common feature in the southern chateaux in the eighteenth century. Marcellin de Marbot, a General in Napoleon's army, told the story in his autobiography of how as a child he crawled through one when he was pretending to be a cat and almost suffocated himself before he was rescued!

The cat flap, in fact, is a practical solution to the age-old dilemma of the cat, poised between domesticity and the call of the wild woods outside; it is also a recognition that the cat is indeed an honoured guest to come and go as he pleases, if not by his own front door, then certainly by the back.